The Amazing
Sunny Colt
Stories

By

Raj & Lavanya

The Amazing Sunny Colt Stories
Copyright © 2018 RJ Publications

http://sunnycolt.com/

Published by RJ Publications

Cover Art by Raj

ISBN: 9780473429959

EISBN: 9780473429973

Fallen Angels

Somewhere burning hunger kept a little girl awake
When we were losing sleep for a toy's sake

Somewhere two tender feet walked on stones
When we were crying for gifts we couldn't own

Somewhere in rags, a girl hid her shame
When buying new clothes was our favourite game

Somewhere tears were flowing just to survive
When we were crying to make dreams alive

Somewhere we read about a silent tear
but lost in our world, we couldn't hear

We can make a difference even in a small way
because somewhere is not very far away

--- Lavanya ---
www.poemsland.com

DEDICATION

Dedicated to our kids Sneha & Shiva
and
All the children of the world
who love bedtime stories

ACKNOWLEDGEMENTS

Our sincere thanks to the kid's school librarian for reviewing and providing feedback. Thanks to a big group of little readers, our children's friends, who read the stories and gave valuable suggestions.

Thanks to our daughter Sneha for submitting the last story of this book, "Sunny and Mrs. Lazy".

Thanks to all our well-wishers for their support and encouragement to publish our first book in the series. We hope to entertain children with more bed time stories of Sunny Colt adventures and we encourage children to submit their stories to us which will be included in our book.

CONTENTS

SOUTHERN FARM'S EXTRAORDINARY COLT

Spring is a superb time to pay a visit to Southern Farms, the biggest animal sanctuary in New Zealand. The melody of chirping birds and the sounds of farm animals create a music that stirs the soul. The farm is a relaxing haven away from the noisy city. Tourists love to visit Southern Farms where lots of fun activities await the kids.

Horseback rides, sheep shearing, and education tours attract kids while adults love to have picnics near the beautiful lakes filled with lotus flowers. Weekends and public holidays are particularly busy, and the farm animals love the attention they get from the kids who feed them. Southern Farms had good facilities and was the perfect place to raise the best breed of farm animals.

That Sunday was busy as usual at Southern Farms. Dr. Julie, the Veterinary Intern was feeling sad because her favourite colt, Sunny was to be sold. The owners decided that Sunny was a liability as he was never picked for a ride. Sunny lived at the back of the farm and wasn't part of the farm's chaotic routine. He felt that he was unlucky to be an ugly colt. He never had any visitors.

The only visitor Sunny had was Dr. Julie.

She went to see Sunny regularly and talked to him about her day. She was sure Sunny understood every word. "It seems as if we have always been friends," thought Julie. Sunny was her good friend and she was heartbroken that Sunny was being sent away from the farm.

Julie saw Tyrone Jones the Farm's Supervisor going on his rounds, looking over the Farm. She ran to see him, hurrying to match his speed, "Mr Jones," she said. "Sunny is the fittest of all the ponies. Please don't send him away." She looked pleadingly at him and silently prayed that he would consider her request.

"Yes Julie, I know that, but our ponies are here for our guests and no one ever picks Sunny. You know that we can't continue to keep a pony who can't entertain the guests. He is becoming a liability for us ." He stopped short of calling Sunny ugly, since he knew that Julie loved him. He recalled the night of Sunny's birth. There was a terrible thunderstorm that night, with lots of lightning that flashed and lit up the barn where Sunny's mother was trying to bring him into the world. The hard delivery sadly resulted in the death of the mare, who died shortly after the colt was born.

He would never forget that even with the sadness of the mare's death, the morning of Sunny's birth went from the darkness of the thunderstorm to a bright, beautiful sunny morning with a lovely rainbow over the farm.

The Farm's senior veterinarian, Dr.Jim Baker was relieved to see that at least the little colt could be saved. "Well, it looks like we are being treated to a beautiful sunrise to replace the darkness of last night's thunderstorm. Let's call this little colt Sunny". Sunny grew up healthy and happy. He was a very friendly horse. But, he was not very handsome and usually none of the kids picked him to ride. Mr. Jones knew Julie loved Sunny and she wouldn't stop pleading her case. Later that day she came into the Farm's office and told him, "I want to take Sunny home when I finish my Internship in three weeks. I am planning to live with my mum on her farm. She needs my help. I spoke to her and we both want Sunny to stay with us."

Mr. Jones knew Julie loved Sunny and would take better care of the colt than anyone else. He agreed to let her take him home. He knew that Julie would be a great vet one day because all the animals at the farm adored her and trusted her completely.

Julie was thrilled and ran to tell Sunny that she is going to take him home with her.

She ran to him saying, "I am taking you home! We can live together now." Julie hugged Sunny. "You will love my mum and her farm, I just know it!".

Sunny was thrilled that he would live with Julie at her farm. She was his favourite person in the whole world. He felt like he had won the best possible prize. "I think this is how it feels to be picked up for a ride!" thought Sunny. "I can never repay Julie", though Sunny, "I will give her lots of love forever."

The weather was a mix of rain and shine in the morning, but late afternoon a bright sun shined in the sky and seemed to touch the farm with sunrays, stopping to say goodbye to Sunny. The little colt watched the sky and thought, "It must be a sign from my mum that everything is going to be ok." Sunny was afraid for a moment thinking of the future, as he never left the farm since his birth. Then he realized that all he needed was Julie's love. It didn't matter if he was going to a strange place. He loved Julie with all his heart. Suddenly, he didn't mind that he was not good looking, and no one picked him for a ride. Nothing mattered now. It was time to put the past behind and look forward to a great future with Julie at her farm.

For a second, Sunny felt like he was bursting with love and joy. He felt like his hooves were not touching the ground and he was floating in the air. Julie, who came to meet him, hugged him close, bursting with joy at the thought that she would be able to give Sunny a new life at her farm. She wanted to capture that moment and snapped a photo of them, against the backdrop of a beautiful rainbow. Julie looked at the photo to check how it looked and was shocked at the result. Snuggled up with her in the photo was the most handsome colt she had ever seen. Sunny's body was glowing and seemed to be floating in the rays of sunshine.

Julie was in a state of shock! How could this have happened? Everyone thought Sunny was the ugliest colt in the farm, but here he was in this photo looking like the most beautiful and magical animal she had ever seen. Julie realized that Sunny was not just an ugly colt like everyone else believed. He was magic and special like she had always known. She didn't tell anyone else about what happened. She didn't want anyone else to find out, and she understood that no one else was able to see Sunny in this special way except her. When she looked at the photo again, it changed back into the way Sunny really looked! Julie felt that her love had caused the change, and she didn't care about anything else except Sunny.

Whether he was magic or not, it would make no difference at all. She was anxious to take Sunny to her mum's farm and wanted the next three weeks to fly by. She couldn't wait to go home and taste her mum's cooking again.

In the next three weeks she saw Sunny as much as possible, and even though the magical change in Sunny's appearance never happened again, she was eager to finish the internship and take Sunny home.

Finally, the big day arrived, and it was full of sunshine and happiness. Julie was thrilled, and it seemed that the sun was shining brighter that day as if it was sending a message from Sunny's mother.

THE MAGIC EYEGLASSES

Julie and Sunny colt started a new life at her mum's farm. Julie loved the place and remembered her childhood, climbing trees and going on horseback rides. She loved nature and animals. Her passion to take care of the animals at her farm inspired her to become a vet. She lost her father when she was 13.

Her mum took care of her and the farm since then. As she grew up, Julie promised herself to help her mother and support her at the farm. The fact that she is a vet now would be a big help to her mum as she could take care of the farm animals.

Julie was concerned about her mother's health as she found out that she was having trouble with her vision. She tried different models of glasses, but none were helping. Julie was worried that her mum's vision would get worse if something was not done but she was not sure how she could help.

She shared her concerns with Sunny. "I wish I

could do something about it. Mum's vision is going from bad to worse. She is trying to hide it from me as she doesn't want me to worry about her. Sunny whole heartedly wished that he could help Julie in some magical way, but he didn't know what he could do.

One day Julie found her mum searching for something. She asked her what she was looking for, but her mum didn't want to bother her. "No worries, honey, I will find it," she said. Julie persisted. "Mum, please let me help. Let me know what you are looking for."

Her mum started crying, "My vision is not as good as it used to be", she admitted. "Now I can't even find my glasses."

Sunny suddenly could hear everything Julie's mum was saying. He was in the back yard away from the home, but his love for Julie and his yearning to protect them gave him the magical power to sense their feelings. His loving heart gave him the power to listen to the words of his loved ones, though he was away from them. He knew that Julie's mum was searching for her glasses and he knew that she won't find them as she forgot them at the library. Sunny concentrated on the power of his magical love and thought, "I can create a special pair of glasses which will never break and adjust to her vision."

As Sunny concentrated with positive thoughts, a brilliant ray of sunshine appeared suddenly, shining through the window. Julie was searching everywhere for the glasses when the sunrays touched her face and moved on to point to the spare bedroom.

"Oh," Julie thought, "Let me search in that room". She went into the spare bedroom and saw that the sun was shining on a shelf. She found a little gift box and opened it to find a letter to her mum. It said, "Dear Customer. We have developed a new pair of glasses that you would be interested in trying. The lens is made of a very special type of adjustable glass. They can be worn under all circumstances from sun to shade and are even great for improving night vision. They can be worn indoors and outdoors and will adapt to the environment.

The best thing about these glasses is that you will never have to go to the doctor again for a replacement. Please try them and let us know what you think.

Thank you

Magical Eyeglasses Inc.

Julie couldn't believe her eyes, "Mum, Mum, look what I found! Amazing glasses which will solve all your problems. Come and see!"

Julie's mum was confused, "I don't remember ordering those glasses!", she said.

"Try them out mum," Julie said. "Maybe they will solve your vision problems. This letter says they are good for everything from reading to driving and night vision!"

Julie's mum was unsure, "I don't know Julie, I didn't order for these glasses. I don't know how they got here and I don't want to experiment with them. Can we just look for my old glasses?", she said.

Julie pleaded with her mum. "I looked everywhere for your glasses. Why not give these new ones a try? Please!"

Her mum reached for the letter and the glasses. She put them on and read the letter. She looked up at Julie and said, "I don't want to waste time telling some overseas company if I like their new product! Just help me find my old glasses."

"Mum," Julie said excitedly. "You read the letter! Those glasses are good. You could read the letter easily!"

Her mum suddenly realized what she had done.

"Wow. Yes, I really did. This is great! I never had such clear vision. Now I can write the farm maintenance article due to be submitted to the local newspaper."

"Good luck on that article," said Julie. "Please also write a review for those glasses. They are great."

"I sure will," said her mum. "Thanks honey."

Sunny was watching everything with his magic vision. He was happy he could help Julie's mum. He began to understand that his love for Julie and the kindness she showed by adopting him kindled some special powers in him. He was no ordinary colt now. He was magical. Sunny vowed to use his magic powers to help not just Julie but anyone who needed help. After all, what else could he do. He had to pass on the good will he received from Julie and share it with the world.

THE HEALING BRACLET

Jack and Sally were kind kids. The siblings loved animals and always wanted to help them. They loved feeding birds and stray animals and always made sure there was water and bird feed in their garden.

Sunny, the magic colt had been watching them for many days and wanted to gift them for their kindness. One day when the kids were feeding the birds in their garden they found a parcel wrapped in golden yellow paper. They were surprised and thrilled to find a letter addressed to them. The letter said - Dear Jack and Sally, you are gifted with special bracelets to acknowledge the kindness you show to the birds and animals who visit your garden every day. These bracelets can heal injuries and cure diseases when you sincerely wish for someone's recovery. You just need to use their healing rays along with have a loving heart and positive feelings. You can harness the magical powers of the bracelets and help injured or sick birds and animals to get well. I am sure you will use them wisely.

From Sunny

Wow," the kids said. "Thanks, Sunny ☺ we will try our best to put them to good use."

The next day, the two children woke up early, ate breakfast and went out to feed the birds that usually came to their garden every morning. There were several ducks, geese and other birds waiting for their regular breakfast. The kids fed them corn, seeds and bird feed and the air filled with the music of happy chirping and quacking. Jack noticed that one of the ducks appeared to be lame. The poor bird had an injured leg. The two children felt very sad watching the bird hopping on one leg, struggling to get its share of the food. They remembered the magical bracelets that Sunny had given them. Jack and Sally touched their magic bracelets and made a sincere wish that the duck should be healed. The duck seemed to trust Jack as he picked it up and held it gently in his lap. Sally touched the duck's hurt leg, and they prayed sincerely that the injured leg should be healed.

Suddenly they noticed a bright golden ray come out of their bracelets. It beamed down on the injured leg and bathed it in brilliant light which glowed like the sunshine. It was as though the bracelets have taken some healing properties from the sun which was not discovered until now. The two children concentrated as hard as they could and suddenly saw that the duck started glowing! It looked like the most beautiful duck they have ever seen.

The ray of sunshine disappeared, and the duck leaped to the ground, completely healed, looking younger and healthier than before. The bracelets worked their magic! The kids thanked Sunny in their mind. This was a miracle! They could help so many birds and animals with this healing power. Jack and Sally promised to themselves that they will make good use of the magic bracelets. They could understand that this was just the beginning. They were chosen to heal many more birds and animals. "Thank You Sunny", they said to themselves, "We will make sure that your magic bracelets will be put to good use".

Sunny was watching them all the while through his magic vision. He was happy that the duck was healed. The kids truly deserved the magic bracelets, Sunny thought. The care and love they had for animals made them eligible to have a special gift like the bracelets, which harnessed the power of sunshine to heal. Sunny was happy that he could help others through his magic powers. After all, any power is great only if it is useful for others in some way.

~

THE SMARTART KIT

Sunny and Julie were excited to host a special lunch for family and friends.

It was a marvellous family reunion. The kids were playing, adults were talking, and the atmosphere was lively and vibrant. Sunny loved the positive vibes filling the home with love. Suddenly he noticed one of the kids sitting in a corner, looking sad. At the same time, Julie noticed the little kid, who was Jimmy, her cousin. "Mum," Julie said, "Why is little Jimmy sad and sitting alone in a corner?". Julie's mother said, "Jimmy is sad because he saw an amazing art kit which he wanted to buy but his parents told him that they can't afford it. You know how hard it is for your uncle to make ends meet. They know that Jimmy is a natural artist but unfortunately, they can't support his dreams. I am sure Jimmy will still become a great artist one day".

"Oh" Julie said, "I will try my best to help Jimmy. Is there anything we can give him to cheer him up?".

Julie's mum shook her head. "Nothing I can think of."

Sunny watched Jimmy from his barn. He couldn't see a sweet kid like Jimmy look sad and lost. He thought, "I will make a magical art kit for him. Something which will cheer him up and help him to bring out the best of his art!"

Julie encouraged Jimmy to go for a walk around the farm so that the animals will distract him and cheer him up. Sunny knew that this was his chance to help. He closed his eyes and concentrated hard, using his magical powers as Jimmy came closer.

A ray of sunshine suddenly beamed down near Jimmy. There in the grass, right where a golden sunray touched the earth, Jimmy found a colourful wrapped box which was addressed to him. Who could have left it here in the field? Jimmy was puzzled.

He ran back into the house, panting with excitement, to show the box to Julie.

"I found this colourful box in the field near Sunny's barn and it has my name on it! What do you think it is? Who could have left it for me?",said Jimmy, unable to hide his excitement.

Jimmy opened the parcel with trembling hands, hoping that it would be something he loves, maybe an art kit. He was disappointed to see something which looked like an iPad. Jimmy was not interested in gadgets. He loved art and he hoped that he could get some art supplies so that he can practice and improve his drawing skills.

Julie saw his disappointed face and said, "Well, let's see what it is."

They took it out of the box, read the instructions and were surprised to see that it was not an iPad but a very special "Art Pad". It was not something found in any shops. Julie never heard of an Art Pad before. The instructions said that it used solar power and the batteries could be recharged. The letter said that it was a special gift for Jimmy as he really loved art and the Art Pad would help him to draw better.

Jimmy took it out of the box. He was curious and started pressing the buttons on the pad. Suddenly something started to project out of the pad like a hologram. "Wow, what's that?" he said. Julie read the instructions and said, "The instructions say that it has a camera and a projector of some sort. You can use it to take a picture of whatever you want to draw." She picked up something that looked like a pencil. "This is like an electronic pencil that can draw and colour." She handed it to Jimmy.

Jimmy started to experiment with the Smart Art Kit. "Wow," he said. "I can pick the style, colour and thickness of the lines. Whatever I draw gets saved and I can pick from all kinds of options, like water colours or oil paints! It has lots of different shades and brush strokes to choose from!"

Jimmy was thrilled. He could hardly wait and was excited to try out his gift. "This is so cool. I am going to start using it right now!"

He pressed another button. "It also has an audio input and I can talk to the Art pad to follow my instructions. This is great."

Sunny watched Jimmy, busy drawing on his new Art Pad. Jimmy was thrilled. He will never need a canvas or art material again. The Art Pad had everything inbuilt and he could create beautiful drawings anywhere, anytime he wanted.

Suddenly a ray of sunshine beamed down on Jimmy. It touched the screen on his Art pad and bounced into rainbow shades, reflecting on the barn where Sunny lived. Jimmy saw Sunny appear into the range of the projector. "Cool" said Jimmy.

"Sunny looks great in the middle of those rainbow colours. I will capture him in my art"

Jimmy finished his drawing quickly and the result was a lovely art of Sunny bathing in rainbow glow.

Sunny watched Jimmy drawing on the Art pad to his heart's content. He was satisfied that once again his unique invention was put to good use.

THE SOOTHING LIGHT

It was Christmas time. Everyone was busy shopping, decorating and celebrating the festive season. Every year the big church in the city hosted a special Christmas party. It was one of the biggest events of the holiday season and thousands of people attended.

Sam and Susie were among the excited kids who came to the Christmas event with their parents. Susie noticed a huge sign put up near the front of the park where the event was being held. The sign had bright red letters which read "Lost children."

Susie thought for a minute and said, "Does it mean that lost children can report here that they are lost or do parents report here about lost children?".

Her brother laughed. "Both! If we get lost and can't find our parents, we can come here, and they will announce our parent's names to come and pick us up. Our parents can also come here if they can't find us. Our names will be announced then, to let us know that we can come here".

The kids were super excited to check out all the stalls as fast as they can. Susie was keen on face painting and was hoping to get a beautiful butterfly design on her cheek. Sam was eager to ride little racing cars. He loved doing the rounds in the car, feeling all grown up. Soon, it was time for the stage performances. Everyone gathered near the stage, and many kids sat on their parent's shoulders to get a good view of the stage show. Sam and Susie noticed a couple who looked upset and worried. They were searching for their son, asking everyone if they had seen a young boy wearing jeans and a yellow shirt.

The kids felt sad for the parents who lost their son. They sincerely wished that they could help. Sam suddenly remembered that his friend Jimmy told him that he was gifted a unique Art pad at his aunt's farm. "I wish I had some gadget to find the little boy", Sam thought. Sam's sincere wish reached Sunny colt. He knew that it was time for him to offer help. Sunny concentrated on his powers and focused on granting Sam's wish.

Suddenly, Sam found a flash light near his feet which was glowing brightly. He picked it up and saw that it had various settings. There was a piece of paper under the flash light which had the instructions. It was a unique flash light which could identify moods. It was a great tool to identify hidden feelings and offer support. If you shine it on a person who is sad it would turn blue and if someone is angry or hurt, it would turn red. Sam shined the flash light on the parents of the missing boy and the light turned blue as they were upset and worried for their kid.

Susie said, "Wow this works! But how can we find the lost kid with this flash light?"

Sam told her, "We can use this flashlight to look for the lost kid. All the kids here are happy and enjoying. If the flash light turns blue on a kid, we can be sure that he is sad and maybe the lost kid.

The kids requested their parents to help them to find the lost boy. However, their parents did not believe that the flash light would change colours according to moods. You see, magic happens only if you believe in it.

Sam and Susan's parents were very practical and were not willing to believe that there are many things in the world which cannot be explained. Of course, they are in for surprise today.

Suddenly Susie said, "Look, the light is slowing changing into a blue shade. I think the lost kid is nearby". Sam said, "Yes. I think the light is indicating that the lost boy is not far away.

Suddenly the light turned completely blue, as the flash pointed towards a little boy who was running around, as if he was searching for someone. "It's the lost kid! shouted Sam. "Come, let's go to him".

They rushed to the little kid and told him that his parents were searching for him. The little kid was extremely happy and started crying. He thought that he would never see his parents again. Everyone went to the lost kids tent and requested the person in charge to announce that the lost kid is found.

The boy's parents rushed to the tent and hugged their son tightly. "We can't thank you enough", they said to Sam and Susie. We thought we would never find our son. How did you find him in this huge crowd?". Sam showed them the flashlight and told them how it worked. The Security In-charge at the lost kids tent found the flash light fascinating and useful. He said, "Could you please give it to our security company. It would really help us on the job". Sam looked at Susie to know her opinion. He knew that it was a unique flash light which would work only if you have positive thoughts. He told the security guard, "I wish I could give it to you, but it works with goodwill and unless you truly care for the other person it won't work". The security guard laughed and said "Well that's hard then. I don't believe in magic. I believe in hard work". The kids knew that they can't give the flash light to the security. It was a unique gift meant for them and it was now their responsibility to make good use of it.

Susie said, "My mum and dad gave me a card to keep in pocket always. It has their phone numbers on it. If I get lost, I can use it to ask someone to call them."

The boy's parents agreed that it was a great idea and they would give their son a little card which had their phone numbers. They thanked Sam and Susie and invited them to visit and have a play date with their son.

Sam and Susie beamed with joy that they could help find a lost kid. They felt like super heroes and then they remembered a famous sentence from the movie Spiderman which says, "With great power comes great responsibility". They knew that the flash light gave them the power to read the inner moods of people. This would be a great tool to find out if someone was unhappy so that they can be supported before they became very depressed. Sam and Susie promised to themselves that they would put the flash light to good use. Sunny colt saw everything through his magical vision. He thought, "Good, another unique gadget has fallen in the right hands. This is my gift to the next generation who are going to change the world with their kind hearts". Sunny's aim was to create an army of miracle workers who would make the world a better place. He knew that the next generation would work for peace not for success, as no one can enjoy a successful life when the world is not at peace".

THE ALL IN ONE CAMP GEAR

Once a month, Julie takes Sunny to visit kids with special needs. It fills her heart with joy watching the kids ride Sunny and have a great time. However, she never knew that Sunny was giving them more than just a good time. He sensed the hopes and wishes of kids who are good at heart and granted their wishes. He put his magic to good use, making sure that their lives are filled with joy.

One bright morning, Sunny was at a local school where all the children were about to go on a camp for one night. He noticed a little girl, Emily sitting in a corner with a sad face.

Sunny read her mind and realized that she was sad because she could not go to the camp. Emily didn't have a sleeping bag, which was a compulsory item for the nature camp. Her parents were on a tight budget, trying their best to feed the kids and meet the expenses. She could not ask her parents and she could not borrow from her friends as all them were also going to the camp.

Sunny decided to use his magic to get Emily a unique sleeping bag. He knew that Emily was a kind kid who was always willing to help others. Sunny concentrated on his magic powers and a bright sunbeam appeared in front of Emily's door, leaving a bright gift box for Emily.

Sunny thought to himself, "Emily will love this unique sleeping bag. I am glad that she will be able to go to the nature camp. I am sure she would learn a lot, discovering the insects and that birds she only saw in her books.

When Emily reached home, she found the gift box at the door step and thought,

"Wow, a gift for me? Who could have left it here?"

Emily rushed inside and said "Mum, mum, look someone sent me a gift and it's not even my birthday! I wonder what it is". She eagerly tore the package, unable to hide her enthusiasm.

Inside, was a beautiful bright sleeping bag which had the shades of a rainbow. "Oh wow, it's beautiful!" Emily said. It was exactly what she wanted to go the camp and it was more beautiful than she could ever imagine. It was as though some super power had listened to her prayers and granted her wish. She was thrilled and could not believe her eyes.

Suddenly, someone knocked on the door.

It was Emily's friend Sam. "Hi Emily," he said, "I asked my cousin to lend you her sleeping bag. I don't want you to miss the trip."

"How nice of you Sam!" Emily's mum said,

"You are very kind, but Emily just received a beautiful sleeping bag as a wonderful surprise gift. Come in. Check it out."

Emily said, "Look Sam, a beautiful sleeping bag which has rainbow shades. I am so happy! I don't know who sent it, but I wish I could just give them a huge hug and say Thank You!

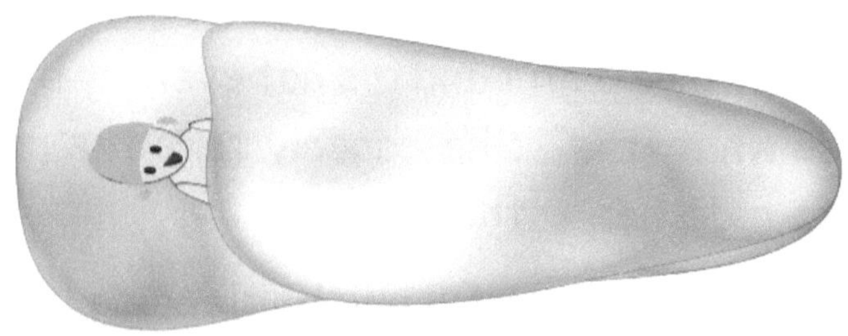

Sam peeped into the bag and said "There is a letter inside. I wonder what it says".

Emily eagerly grabbed the letter and said, "Hey let me read it. I want to know who sent it".

"Dear Emily", the letter said, "You are such a kind girl, always trying to help others. I would like to reward you for your kindness by giving you this sleeping bag, which will be useful for your trip. I would be glad if you could pay it forward and make someone else happy within a week.

Your magical friend – Sunny

Emily was very happy that she was chosen to get a special gift. She promised to herself that she will repay her magical friend's kindness by giving joy to someone else. "But what can I do", she said, "I am just a little girl who doesn't have money to buy a nice gift for someone". Sam said, "Emily, you don't need to give a gift to make someone happy. Being kind itself if a big gift which you already give others. That's why you are my best friend". Emily was filled with joy hearing Sam's words. "Thanks a lot Sam! You are always kind to me too".

Emily's dad who was listening to the kids said "Emily, you could just help your mum with house work and give her some time to relax on the couch. That's a big gift you can give her as she is always so tired coming home from work. I am sure she will really appreciate it". "Of course," said Emily's mum, "Would you like to help me set the table for lunch and later fold some clothes for me". "Sure, Mum", said Emily. She was thrilled that she was getting a chance to repay the help she received from someone who gifted her the sleeping bag. "Thank you Sunny", she silently thanked her magical friend. At the farm, Sunny was thrilled to see what happened, Wow! Another wish fulfilled for a little girl, and the best part is that she paid it forward and helped someone else, which is great. The world would be such a great place if everyone did that!

THE ODOUR DETECTOR

One day Sunny went to the school near the farm to see if any of the kids need his help. He turned himself into a toy horse so that he could stand in a corner and observe everyone.

Sunny heard the kids complain about a strange smell and he triggered his magic hearing to listen to the conversation. He heard Susie say "That strange smell is making me feel sick. I wish we could find where it's coming from". Max agreed, "Yes, it's getting worse day by day. The janitor could not find anything in the class and all of us are finding it hard to sit in the class. If the weather was better, we could have sat under the trees instead of sitting in the class and bearing that awful smell".

Susie said, "Yes, we must find out the cause of that strange smell so that the kids don't fall sick".

The kids were on the way home and as the bus reached home they saw golden sunbeams bending to touch the earth.

Max reached home first and saw a bright colourful gift box on the doorstep. It was addressed to him and it was from his Science Club. He rushed inside shouting, "Mum, Mum, look, I got something from my Science Club."

At the same time Susie reached home and she too found a gift on her doorstep. She was super excited and called Max to share the news. They eagerly waited to meet at school the next day to show each other their surprise gifts.

At last, during morning tea break, they got a chance to share their gifts. "Look, I got a telescope from my Science club", Max said, "The letter says that it's a unique telescope that helps you find hidden things".

Susie was thrilled, "That sounds cool, we need to test it out. Look what I got in my giftbox. The note says it's an odour detector to locate smells! It works like a compass, but it shows where smells are coming from, instead of just showing directions."

"Hey," said Susie, "Let's use the apple core I found in the garden. We can hide it and then use the telescope and the smell detector to find it."

They hid the apple and tested their gadgets.

The smell detector arrow pointed exactly to the tree where they hid the apple core.

Max looked through the telescope, he could see the apple. Both the gifts worked perfectly, and the kids were excited at the possibilities of what they could do with them.

Max and Susie had a bigger plan to make good use of their gadgets. They wanted to detect the source of the strange smell in their classroom and get to the bottom of the mystery before everyone got sick.

Susie used her smell detector to find the location of the strange smell. "It's in that direction," she shouted pointing to the book cupboard. They searched in the cupboard but could not find anything but books.

Max said, "Wait, let's try my telescope. Maybe there is something hidden that we can't see." He took out his telescope and carefully scanned the inside of the cupboard. Suddenly Max yelled out, "I see something! It is behind the cupboard."

Max ran to their teacher, "Mrs Thomas, we have found the source of the strange smell. It looks like something is jammed behind the cupboard. Can you please help us to move the cupboard away from the wall, so we can see what it is?"

At last, the stinky secret was revealed. There was a rotten sandwich stuck to the wall behind the cupboard. Mrs. Thomas couldn't believe her eyes, "Holy Moly! I wonder how that sandwich got behind the cupboard? Well done kids! You solved the stinky smell mystery. I will make sure you get rewarded at the school assembly on Monday with special star badges and certificates".

Max and Susie were thrilled. They knew that getting a star badge and a certificate from the Principal would be a great honour and it would add to their year end review.

Their faces beamed with joy. Suddenly golden yellow sunrays came through the class room window and shined brightly on them.

Max and Susie felt a burst of joy and kindness in their hearts. They looked at each other and smiled. It was as though they were on the same wave length and could read each other's thoughts. Max said "Mrs. Thomas could we donate our gadgets to the school so that everyone can make use of them even in the future." "Yes Mrs. Thomas, said Susie, "There is only so much we can do on our own. I am sure the Principal and all the teachers will make sure that our gadgets can be used for science experiments and discovering new things".

"Well done kids", said Mrs. Thomas. "You not only helped us identify the source of the stink but donated your gadgets to the school. We need more kids like you. I am sure your kindness will spread to your friends and you will make the school a better place". Sunny heard the teacher's words through his magical senses and was filled with joy. Another problem solved and the icing on the cake was that the kids decided to donate their gifts to the school. Sunny was happy that he made the right choice by gifting the unique telescope and odour detector to Max and Susie. Kids who share their gifts with others set a good example to everyone around them.

THE HERBAL HEALER

Sid and Rose were late for school that day and missed the roll call. Rose tried to rush ignoring the sharp pain on her forehead. She tripped on a rock earlier and hurt her forehead. She couldn't wait to go to the school office to show the nurse.

Rose's Mum was called in to take her home. The cream which the doctor gave some relief, but the mark on her forehead did not go away even after a few months. Her mother wished that the mark would go away with time, but it looked like the mark would stay forever.

Rose did not bother about the mark on her forehead but one day she was in a school play in the lead role and she truly wished she didn't have the mark on her face. The sincere wish from Rose's heart reached Sunny. He knew that she needed something magical to heal her.

One Sunday afternoon Rose was sleeping in her bedroom watching out of the window. Golden yellow daffodils danced in the sunshine and Rose was filled with joy watching them.

Suddenly a brilliant yellow sunbeam came down and touched their post box. Rose saw her mother go out and collect the post. Her mother rushed excitedly into her room holding a small parcel. "Look Rose! There is a parcel for you. I am sure this will cheer you up".

Rose opened the box with great enthusiasm. She was feeling very sad since the injury and receiving a gift was the best thing which happened to her. The golden yellow box had some cream inside it. The label read "Sunny Aloe Vera Cream – Cures all skin marks like magic. Made from natural herbal ingredients. Sample sent for review."

"Mum", Rose said, "We used some very good creams which the doctor gave but still the mark didn't go away. Do you think this cream will help?". "I don't know baby", Rose's mother said. "I never tried herbal products before. Let me browse and read about Aloe Vera so that we know that it's safe". They researched on the internet and found that the Aloe Vera plant has great healing benefits. "Wow, I never imagined that herbal products can be so good", said Rose's mum. True to its word, the cream worked its magic and the mark disappeared very soon. Rose's mum thanked the sender silently in her mind.

Sunny was happy that the herbal cream not only healed Rosie but also helped to promote herbal products which are good in every way. They are not made with chemicals which can have serious side effects. Sunny knew that Rose and her mother would now promote herbal products among their family and friends. Sunny hoped that one day the world would discover the magical healing properties of herbs and stop using chemical based medicines. Sunny was happy that kids like Rose who enjoy the benefits of herbal products will promote them and the next generations will make the world better place by using natural products.

SUNNY AND MRS. LAZY

(SUBMITTED BY A YOUNG READER)

One day Sunny decided to go see Sam and Sally because he knew they were having a playdate. He wanted to see how things were going. Before he got there, Sam and Sally were playing when suddenly they heard a strange noise.

Sally said, "Oh don't worry. That is just my aunt Jane. She is very lazy. Even my mum gets mad at her and it is her own sister! I tried all kinds of things to get her to do more things but all she wants to do is take naps, and that noise is her snoring!"

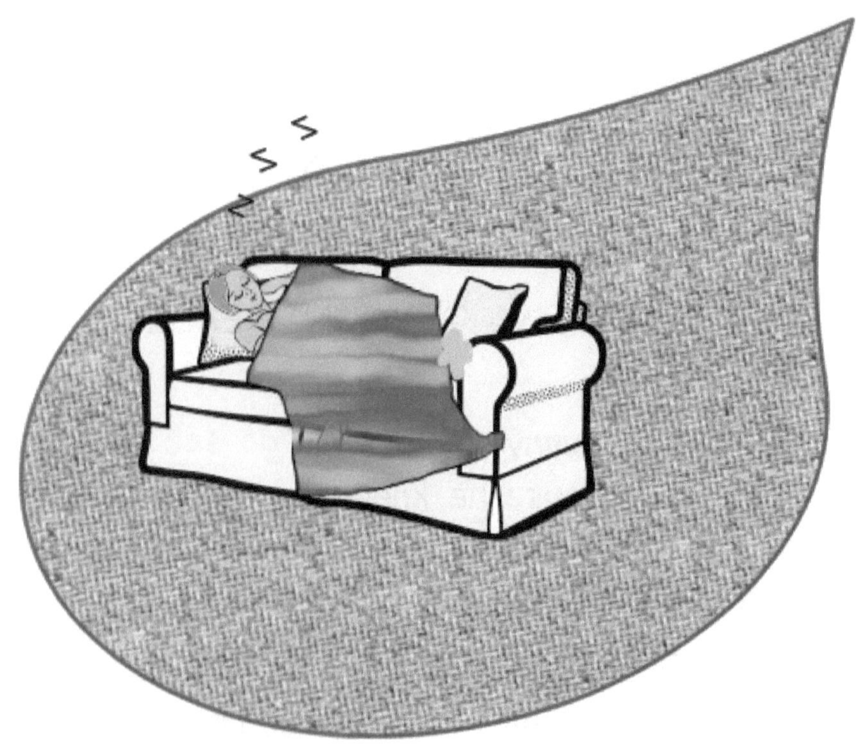

Sam said, "Sorry, I wish I knew a solution to help you get your aunt to do more things and not be so lazy."

Sunny had just gotten to their home and had heard every word of the kid's conversation. He decided to help them to find a way to get Sally's aunt to be more active. He suddenly smiled because he had a great idea.

Sally decided to take a look in their mailbox to see if the mail had arrived. She also noticed a brilliant sunbeam shining right onto their mailbox!

In the box she found a small package that was yellow in colour just like the sunbeam.

She picked up the package and went in the house.

She opened the box, and inside were some instructions, and a strange gadget called a Mind-Altering Machine. She read the instructions. It said that all you had to do in order to change someone's mind was to place the end of the pointer to the person's ear and speak into it and say what you want the person to do next.

Then, the person will do what you say, but it must only be commands for the good of the person, as something like telling them to buy you a present will not work.

The two kids looked at each other, and Sam suggested, "Why don't we try it on your aunt. It really is for her own good as it is bad for your health to be so lazy."

They carefully went over to the couch where her aunt was sleeping and gently pointed the gadget to her ear. Then Sally said, "Auntie, you will get up and go outside and take a walk with us to get some exercise instead of sleeping on the couch."

They waited to see what would happen. Suddenly her aunt woke up and yawned. She said, "Hi kids. Why are you inside on such a nice day? Let's all take a walk in the beautiful sunshine! Don't you see that sunbeam shining on our house?"

Sunny watched them as they came down past his barn, and they, waved at him as they went by. He smiled and the sunbeam slowly faded as the children and Sally's aunt kept walking down the trail.

------------The End------------

~ 49 ~